For my father
— C.R.

A NOTE ABOUT THIS STORY

When a child becomes aware of his or her pending death and is given the opportunity to "draw your feelings," he or she will often draw a blue or purple balloon, released and floating free. Health care professionals have discovered that this is true regardless of a child's cultural or religious background, and researchers believe that it demonstrates the child's innate knowledge that a part of him or her will live forever.

I first heard this moving and fascinating anecdote from the psychiatrist and author of *On Death and Dying*, Elisabeth Kübler-Ross. It has affected me ever since.

—Ann Armstrong-Dailey, Founding Director
and CEO, Children's Hospice International

the Purple Balloon

Chris Raschka

schwartz & wade books · new york

No one likes to talk
about dying.

It's hard work.

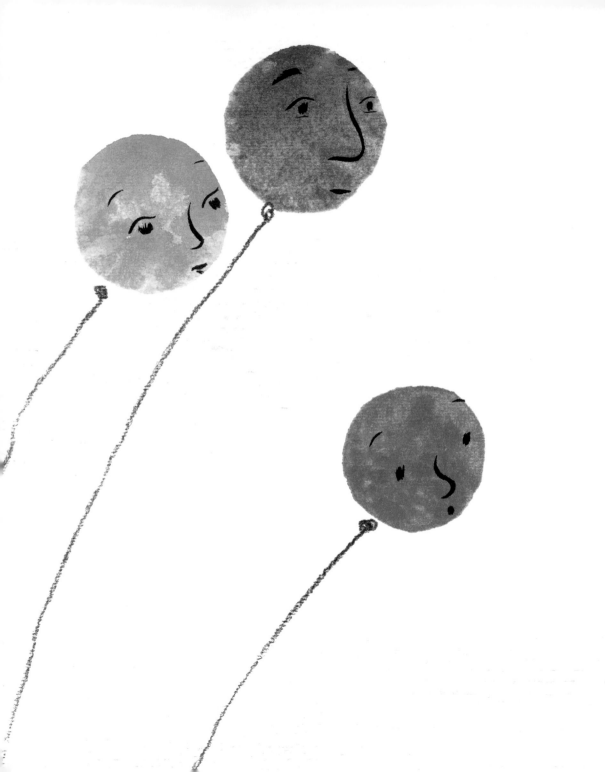

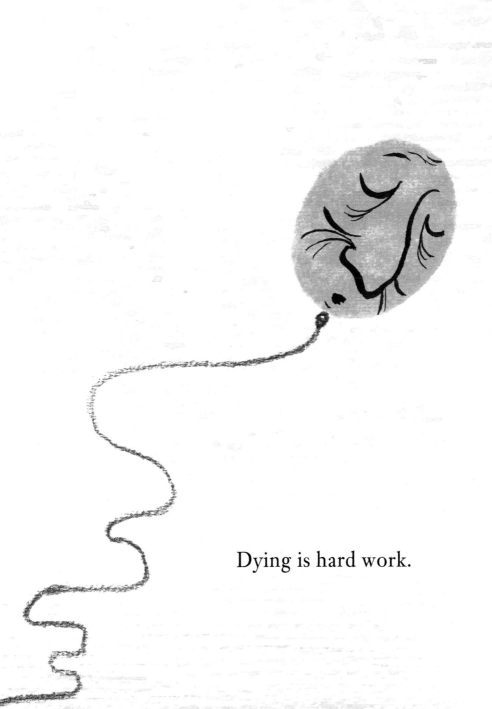

Dying is hard work.

Many people do what they
can to make dying not so hard.

Nurses, doctors, hospice
care workers.

Clergy, friends, neighbors.

Brothers, sisters, nephews,
nieces, grandchildren, sons
and daughters.

Everyone helps

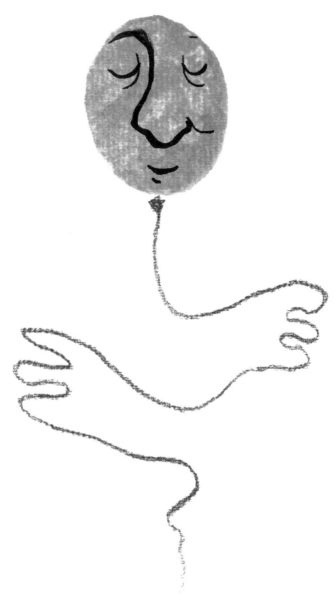

when someone dies.

When someone dies,
it's good to have a family.

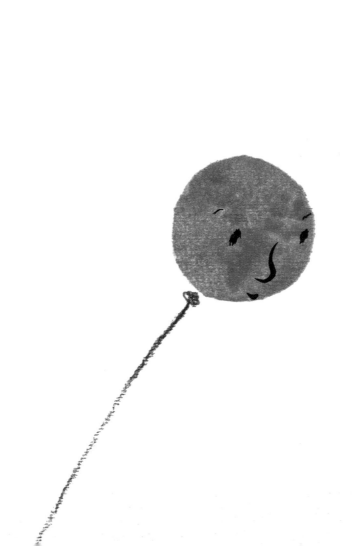

And it's good to have friends.

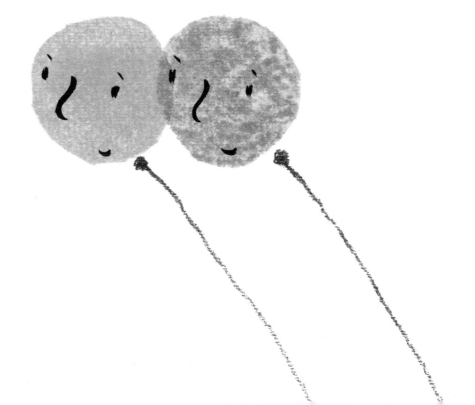

They help you feel better.

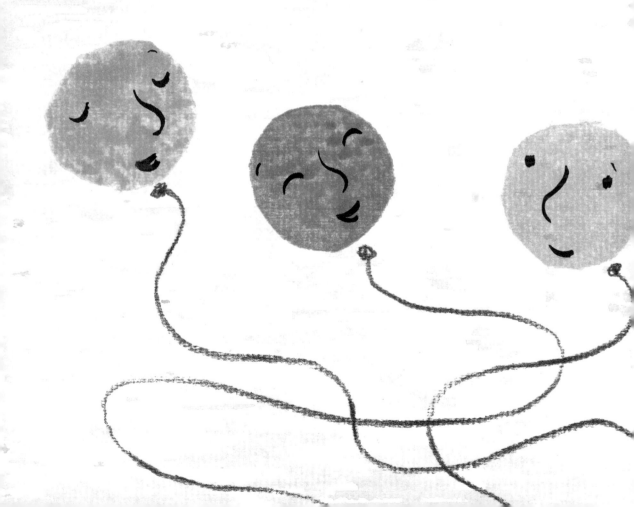

There is only one thing
harder to talk about than
someone old dying—

someone young dying.

Just as many people need to help.

Neighbors and friends and classmates. Hospice care workers, and nurses and doctors and therapists. Teachers and tutors.

Of course, mothers and fathers and sisters
and brothers and uncles and aunts and
cousins and grandparents.

All listening or talking,
sitting or holding, being
noisy or being quiet.

Good help makes
dying less hard.

Good help makes leaving easier.

WHAT YOU CAN DO TO HELP

Continue to be a friend.

Treat your sick friend the same as you treat your other friends:

Don't make a big deal of your friend's illness, even if he or she looks or acts different.

Let your friend know you're there if he or she needs someone to talk to or needs help.

Keep in touch if a friend or classmate is absent from school or in the hospital:

Send a card or an e-mail.

Send a favorite book.

Visit if you can.

Keep your friend informed about what's going on in school, with other friends, etc., including him or her in as many ways as you can.

A portion of the publisher's proceeds will be donated to:

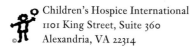 Children's Hospice International
1101 King Street, Suite 360
Alexandria, VA 22314

www.chionline.org

Children's Hospice International (CHI) is a nonprofit organization
dedicated to ensuring medical, psychological, social, and spiritual support
to all children with life-threatening conditions and their families by
providing a network of resources and care.

Copyright © 2007 by Chris Raschka

All rights reserved.
Published in the United States by Schwartz & Wade Books,
an imprint of Random House Children's Books, a division of Random House, Inc., New York.

SCHWARTZ & WADE BOOKS and colophon are trademarks of Random House, Inc.

www.randomhouse.com/kids

Educators and librarians, for a variety of teaching tools,
visit us at www.randomhouse.com/teachers

Library of Congress Cataloging-in-Publication Data

Raschka, Christopher.
   The purple balloon / Chris Raschka. — 1st ed.
      p. cm.
   Summary: Easy-to-read text reveals that dying is hard work, for the old and especially the
young, and how good it is that so many people help when a person dies, from medical staff
to clergy and friends to family members.
   ISBN: 978-0-375-84146-0 (trade) — ISBN: 978-0-375-94259-4 (lib. bdg.)
   [1. Death—Fiction. 2. Terminally ill—Fiction.] I. Title.
PZ7.R1814Pur 2007
[E]—dc22
2006023725

The text of this book is set in Archetype.
The illustrations are potato and wood prints rendered in watercolor paint.

PRINTED IN CHINA

10 9 8 7 6 5 4 3 2 1

First Edition